CHEER CAPTAIN

BY JAKE MADDOX

text by Margaret Gurevich

illustrated by Pulsar Studio
(Beehive)

STONE ARCH BOOKS

Jake Maddox books are published by Stone Arch Books
A Capstone Imprint
151 Good Counsel Drive, P.O. Box 669
Mankato, Minnesota 56002
www.capstonepub.com

*Library of Congress Cataloging-in-Publication Data is available on the
Library of Congress website.*

Library Binding: 978-1-4342-2551-1

Summary: Julia is lucky to already know someone at her new school: her
best friend, Ava. But when both girls try out for the cheerleading squad,
their friendship is put to the test.

Art Director/Graphic Desinger: Kay Fraser
Image Manipulation: Sean Tiffany
Production Specialist: Michelle Biedscheid

Printed in the United States of America in Stevens Point, Wisconsin.
092010
005934WZS11

TABLE OF
★ CONTENTS ★

CHAPTER 1

EVERYTHING YOU KNOW

Sweating, I lay down on the grass and closed my eyes. The hot August sun beat down on my face, but it was still cooler than doing cartwheels.

Ava, my best friend, stood over me. She bounced on her toes. "Get up, lazy bones," she teased. She gently kicked my sneaker with hers. "Come on, Julia. We have a lot of work to do."

I groaned, but I got up.

My family and I had just moved across town to River City East. I'd be starting at a new middle school next week. At my old middle school, I'd been captain of the cheerleading squad. The one thing that would make the move to a new school okay would be joining the cheerleading team.

Luckily for me, my best friend, Ava, had been on the River City East squad for two years. She knew all the moves and had promised to teach me the routines. She'd even loaned me a uniform. All I had to do was try out. But first, I had to practice. That's what we were doing in her backyard.

I was so glad I knew Ava. She had been my best friend since kindergarten. She'd moved to River City East in third grade. Having her at my new school was going to be a huge help. At least I'd know someone.

Ava turned up the volume on her iPod dock and started jumping. "C'mon, Julia. Kick those legs higher," she told me.

"I'm trying," I said, kicking as high as I could. Sweat rolled down my neck.

"Much better," Ava said as I did ten kicks in a row. "Now, onto the Hello cheer. We do that at the beginning of every routine."

I gulped water from my water bottle. Ava smiled at me. "How about you watch me first, okay?" she asked.

I nodded and plopped down in a shady spot. Ava clapped her hands, did a flip, and jumped. She ended the cheer with a split, her arms raised in a high V, pom-poms in her hands.

"Wow, that was great!" I said, clapping.

Ava flashed me a wide smile. "Your turn!" she said.

I took my time getting started. Ava frowned. "Julia, you need to step it up," she said. "Tryouts are in two weeks. More people are trying out this year than ever before. I thought you wanted this."

"You're right," I said. "I'm sorry. Show me everything you know!"

* * *

The rest of the week, Ava and I practiced every day. She helped me nail the clapping rhythm for the Hello cheer, and we motivated each other to jump higher. I didn't complain once.

"You know what would be perfect?" Ava asked on Sunday afternoon. We were taking a snack break on her porch.

"What would be perfect?" I asked, popping a strawberry into my mouth.

"If we both made captain. How awesome would that be? We'd both be responsible for leading the team," she said. She took a big bite out of her strawberry.

"That would be great," I admitted. "But I'm new. I won't be captain."

Secretly, I really wanted to be a captain. But I knew that would be difficult. Just making the squad was going to be hard enough for me.

"Think positive," Ava said. "Everyone — old and new — has a shot." She gave me a hug.

"It's easy for you to think positive," I said. "You've been captain for the past two years. You're really good."

Ava shrugged. "Sure, the coaches know me," she said, "but you're good, too. They'll notice how hard you've been working."

I smiled at her. "You're right," I said. "I just have to keep working hard. Let's get back to practicing!"

CHAPTER 2

FIRST DAY

When I got to my locker on Monday morning, Ava and her friends were already there.

"Hey, Jules!" Ava said. She turned to her friends and said, "This is my best friend, Julia."

Everyone smiled, and most of them said hello. A blond girl wearing sparkly tennis shoes waved but didn't say anything.

"I'm Stefanie," said a short, bouncy girl wearing a headband. "Will you be trying out for the cheer team, too?"

"That's the plan!" I said.

"Great!" Stefanie said.

"Yeah, great," mumbled the blonde.

Stefanie nudged the girl with her elbow. Then she turned to me. "Don't mind Casey," Stefanie said. "She's just worried that another girl trying out will hurt her chances of making captain."

Casey looked down at the floor. "It's a tough competition," she mumbled.

"I'm sure you'll be great either way," I said, smiling at Casey.

"That's what I keep telling her," said Stefanie.

"All right, guys," said Ava. "We'll talk more at lunch. Right now, we better move, or we'll be late to homeroom."

"See you later!" yelled Stefanie as she ran down the hall. Casey waved and walked away.

Ava put her arm around my shoulders. "I told you it wouldn't be so bad," she whispered and then ran after the others.

* * *

That night Mom made my favorite dinner — baked ziti with extra cheese — to celebrate the start of a new school year.

"How was your first day?" she asked as she placed the ziti on the table.

"Better than I thought it would be," I admitted. I scooped pasta onto my plate.

"Make any new friends?" asked Dad.

"A few. One girl, Stefanie, was really nice," I told him. "She even shared her Ho-Hos with me at lunch."

"That's what I like to hear," said Dad. "See? Everything at your new school is going to be great. Nothing to worry about."

When dinner was over, Dad and I helped Mom wash the dishes. Dad got silly and squirted us with the sink nozzle. Mom laughed so hard she snorted. They always made it easy to forget my worries. At least for a while.

That night, as I lay in my bed and stared at my ceiling, I couldn't get the cheerleading tryouts out of my head. One week and counting. I hoped I would make the team. I hoped we all would.

CHAPTER 3

TRYOUTS

"Today's the big day," said Casey at lunch the next Monday. She was finally being friendly to me.

"That's right," I said, picking at my sandwich. I was too nervous to eat.

Stefanie watched as Casey finished her sandwich and fries and started on her cookies. "How can you even eat?" Stefanie asked. "My stomach is doing cartwheels."

"Seriously," said Ava, pushing aside her mac and cheese. "The thought of eating makes me feel sick. I'm so nervous!"

I was happy to know I wasn't the only one anxious about tryouts.

Casey laughed. "I'm nervous too, but I need energy for the tryouts," she explained. "If you guys don't eat you'll be too tired to jump."

Ava threw a fry at Casey.

"More food. Yay!" said Casey, laughing.

Ava giggled but then leaned in, looking serious. "Guys, we should make a pact," she said, looking at each of us. "No matter what happens, we will all support each other. Okay?"

"You got it, Captain," said Stefanie. Ava smiled.

Just before the tryouts, Ava went to a corner to practice her routine one last time. I walked over and touched her shoulder.

"You know the routine perfectly," I said. "You'll do great." Then, because I knew it would make her smile, I added, "Captain."

She did smile. "You're such a good friend, Julia," Ava said, giving me a big hug. "I'm so glad you transferred to this school."

The cheerleading coach, Coach Shue, called for everyone to line up. We all grabbed our pom-poms and stood in a line in front of the judges' table.

"Good luck!" Stefanie whispered.

"Break a pom-pom!" joked Casey, and I heard Ava laugh.

We all stood in front of the judges to perform our routines. Ava went first. My stomach flipped with each of her moves. I wasn't sure if I was nervous for her or for myself.

Ava's voice projected on the Hello cheer, and her cartwheels were great. Then it came time to throw the pom-poms in the air, do a pike jump, land, and catch the pom-poms. Over the summer, Ava had always made it look so easy. I was sure she'd be perfect.

The music got louder. Ava threw her pom-poms high in the air and did her jump. She landed on her feet but missed the pom-pom catch.

"Oh, no," Stefanie whispered, covering her mouth with her hand.

Ava said something to the judges, and they nodded. She put her hands on her hips. It looked like her legs were shaking. "Ready? Okay," she called. Then she tried the move again.

She jumped up and tossed her pom-poms. This time, she didn't slide down completely on the split, and she missed her pom-poms again. As soon as she stood up, Ava ran out of the gym.

"I need to go after her," I said.

Stefanie grabbed my arm. "You can't," she said. "You're next. The rest of her routine was great. I'm sure she'll get in."

Coach Shue called my name. I ran to the table. None of my new friends told me to break a pom-pom. I think they were afraid they would jinx me, too.

CHAPTER 4

WHO'S IN?

"Wow, Julia," said Stefanie when tryouts were over. "You did great. I think that was the highest pike jump I've ever seen."

"Thanks," I said, blushing. I was surprised by how well the routine had gone. I'd even nailed the split without wobbling. "I could never have done any of it without Ava," I added.

"Speaking of," said Casey, as we headed to the locker room. "Where is Ava?"

"Ava?" I called, pushing the locker room door open. I was sure she'd be waiting for us, but no one was there.

Stefanie frowned. "She's probably still upset," she said. "Let's see if she went home."

On the way to Ava's house, Casey and Stefanie chatted about how well all of our routines had gone and how fun it would be to go to the games together. Casey didn't seem worried about making the team anymore.

When we got to Ava's, her mom answered the door.

"Hi, girls," she said quietly, only opening the door halfway. "Ava is a little upset right now, but I'm sure she'll be back to her old self soon."

"Can you tell her we stopped by?" asked Casey. "And that she did a lot better than she thinks."

Ava's mom smiled. "I'll do that," she said. "Ava is lucky to have such caring friends."

"You know what I don't get?" asked Stefanie as we walked away.

"What?" asked Casey.

"She messed up a little, sure. But Ava has been to enough tryouts to know that one mistake won't keep her from making the team. Not if the rest of the routine was as good as hers," Stefanie said.

"Making the team isn't enough for Ava. She wants to be captain, remember?" I said.

"Right," said Stefanie quietly.

"Maybe that can still happen," said Casey, but she sounded unsure.

"Maybe," I said. But deep down, I knew Ava wouldn't be captain.

* * *

The next day at lunch, no one talked about the tryouts. We ate our sandwiches and pudding and laughed about the toupee our science teacher wore.

Ava laughed so hard, milk came out of her nose. I was glad she was feeling better.

Then there was an announcement over the loudspeaker. "Attention, all girls who tried out for cheerleading," said Coach Shue. "Please come to the gym after school to see if your name is on the list."

We all looked at each other. Ava seemed really nervous.

Then she forced a smile. "Sorry for being so worried," she said. "It will be really fun when we're cheering together."

* * *

After school, I tried to see over the crowd of girls already gathered in the gym. Casey pushed to the front of the group. She ran her finger down the names and squealed excitedly. "I'm in! I'm in!" she told us.

Ava, Stefanie, and I made it to the front of the group. "Awesome," said Ava. She scanned the names. "I'm there, too! And you too, Stef!"

Then they all looked at me.

Please be there, I thought.

I read the list three times, but my name wasn't on it. I could feel the tears coming.

"Wait," Stefanie said, lifting the sheet. "There's another page!"

We crowded around the second piece of paper, and I took in a sharp breath. There was my name. I was so happy, I almost didn't see the word underneath it.

In bold letters, it said CAPTAIN.

CHAPTER 5

TIME

The next day, Ava wasn't waiting by my locker when I got to school. I didn't see her at lunch, either.

I sat down at our usual table by myself. I tried to eat my lunch, but no one else showed up. Finally, I gave up and went to the library.

As soon as I walked through the door, I saw Ava, Stefanie, and Casey huddled around a computer.

Stefanie spotted me, smiled, and waved me over.

I breathed a sigh of relief. I'd been so worried that Ava would be upset with me because I was named captain instead of her. And another part of me thought Casey and Stefanie would ignore me, too. I was glad I was wrong.

"Group project for history class," Stefanie said, rolling her eyes.

Ava's eyes didn't leave the computer screen. She mumbled, "Hi."

I sat down beside her. "Did your mom tell you I called last night?" I asked.

"Uh, yeah, but I was so tired," she said. She punched a few keys, and the printer began spitting out pages. Suddenly, Ava stood up.

"Gotta go," she said. "I have to ask my teacher a question."

"See you at practice!" I called.

But Ava was already out the door. She didn't answer.

* * *

By the time cheerleading practice started, I was sure something was wrong. Each time I put my hands on my hips and shouted "Ready? Okay!" to get a cheer started, Ava would be a beat off. That made the whole squad mess up.

After practice, Coach Shue pulled me aside. "You're the captain, Julia," she said. "The girls look to you for direction. If one girl is off, the rest of the group is off, too. Part of your job is to make sure that everyone's doing the cheer right."

What could I say? I didn't want to tell Coach Shue that Ava was messing up because she was upset that she wasn't captain.

So I just nodded and said, "I understand, Coach. I'll do better next practice."

She grinned. "I know you will!" she told me.

At dinner that night, I couldn't stop thinking about it. Something was definitely wrong with my friendship with Ava.

I noticed my mom watching me. "Want to talk about it?" she asked.

I shook my head. I was afraid if I opened my mouth I would cry. "May I be excused?" I asked quietly. I just wanted to go to bed. Maybe by tomorrow, Ava would like me again.

Mom frowned. Then she said, "Sure. But if you want to talk, we're here."

Dad patted my arm and added, "Whatever it is, it will work out. Just give it time."

I hoped he was right.

CHAPTER 6

MISS CAPTAIN

The next day I got to practice early. Coach Shue and the assistant coaches, Coach Crane and Coach Heep, were already there.

"Hi, Julia. I have exciting news to share!" said Coach Shue. "I entered the squad in a competition!"

I squealed and jumped up and down. "Yay!" I said. I'd always wanted to compete. Now I'd get my chance.

Casey, Ava, and Stefanie walked in, and when they heard the news, they began squealing, too. Soon the whole squad was bouncing and doing cartwheels. We were too happy to practice.

Coach Shue blew her whistle, and we quieted down. "The competition is three weeks away," she said. "We have our work cut out for us. Everyone will need to work extra hard now. Is that clear?"

Everyone nodded.

"Great!" Coach Shue said. She clapped her hands. "Now let's get started. Julia will lead us in the Hello cheer. Then Coach Crane, Coach Heep, and I will split you into three groups and teach you the dance routine."

I got up. Stefanie gave me a grin.

"Ready?" I yelled. I placed my hands on my hips. Every other girl did, too. Ava smiled, and that made me feel better. "Okay!" I yelled and began the cheer.

I put my arms in a low V, and Casey followed. I did a toe-touch jump, both legs high in the air on either side of me like a split, and the rest of the squad did, too. The end of the cheer called for a cartwheel, and we each did one.

We all landed firmly on our feet at the same time. I felt energized and happy as we went through the cheer. I put my left arm up in the air, and everyone else did the same.

Well, almost everyone. As we stepped into our places, Ava stumbled forward. The three coaches clapped at the finish and yelled "Bravo!" Ava wasn't smiling, though.

Before we split into our groups, I put my arm around Ava's shoulder. "You only missed one. It's not a big deal," I said, hoping to cheer her up.

"Maybe not to you, Miss Captain," she said. Then she ran to her group, leaving me staring after her.

Casey looked at me but didn't say anything. Then she ran to catch up with Ava.

I didn't understand what had just happened. I felt a light poke on my shoulder.

It was Stefanie. "Ava will get over it," she said.

"What if she doesn't?" I asked.

"She's just hurt," Stefanie said. "I'm sure deep down she knows it's not your fault."

I sighed. "What about Casey? She seems annoyed at me, too."

Stefanie rolled her eyes. "Casey just doesn't want Ava to be mad at her," she said.

"And you don't care if Ava is mad at you?" I asked quietly.

"I care about my friends," Stefanie said. She shrugged. "And you're my friend, too." She gave me a quick hug and added, "Now let's go before Coach Shue gets mad at both of us!"

CHAPTER 7

BACK TO NORMAL

A week later, only Stefanie ate lunch with me. Ava barely said hello when she saw me. Casey only talked to me when Ava wasn't around. Cheerleading practice was going well when the coaches were teaching us the dance routine. But as soon as they asked me to lead, Ava would do something that screwed us all up.

At the end of the week, Coach Shue asked me to stay after practice.

She gave me another speech about being a leader. This time she said if things didn't improve by the end of the following week, she would have to rethink my position as captain.

"Maybe if I wasn't captain everything could go back to normal," I told Stefanie at lunch.

Stefanie frowned. "That wouldn't be good at all!" she said. "You're the captain because you're the best."

"But I'm sick of Ava being mad at me," I said.

"Ava's not the only one on the team," Stefanie told me. "I heard the other girls talking, and they all really like you."

"Maybe Ava could be a good captain, too," I said, staring down at my food.

Stefanie shook her head. "I like Ava, too," she said, "but you're what's best for the team. That's why the coaches picked you. The way Ava is acting isn't fair."

I didn't say anything.

"Let's just see how today's practice goes, okay?" asked Stefanie.

"Okay," I said. I picked up my taco and took a large bite. I'd need all the strength I could get.

* * *

I spotted Ava standing in the corner of the gym before practice started. "Hey," I said shyly.

"Hi," she said.

I took it as a good sign that she didn't ignore me. "I never got the chance to say I was sorry about how everything turned out," I said quietly.

"Yeah," she said. I waited for her to say something else, but she didn't.

"Um, yeah," I began. "About the routine. Do you need help?"

Ava pressed her lips together. "Are you saying I'm not as good as you?" she asked.

"Of course not!" I said. "I'd never —"

Just then, Coach Shue blew her whistle. Ava glared at me. Then she ran to join the other girls.

I had wanted to tell her how much I had appreciated her help this summer. I just wanted to help her, the way she'd helped me. Would I ever get the chance?

"Show us what you got, girls!" said Coach Shue, turning on the music.

We started the dance with everyone standing in line, heads down. As the music grew faster and louder, we picked our heads up and stepped out of the line one by one. Everyone seemed to be right on the beat as we turned cartwheels and made our pyramid.

For the finale, I was lifted to the top of the pyramid. I made a high V with my arms. Then, I was thrown up in the air and caught by a bunch of arms. Perfect!

That only left two more parts. Everyone marched back in the line, just like when the cheer began. On the last note, we put our hands in the air in touchdown position and fell like dominoes.

It was almost perfect. But at the last second, Ava stepped out of line, and the domino part didn't work.

"Not bad at all," said Coach Shue when the music stopped. "Julia, can I please see you for a moment?"

I walked up to Coach Shue. All of the other girls headed into the locker room. I thought I saw Ava glance back at me.

"What did you think of the routine?" Coach Shue asked.

"I thought everyone did a great job," I replied. "We just have to work on the ending a little bit."

Coach Shue nodded. "I think so, too," she told me. "I talked to Ava before practice, and she said she was having a hard time keeping up with you."

I didn't know what to say. Was that true? Was I going too fast? Or was Ava so mad that I was captain, she would say anything? Either way, I knew she wouldn't let me help her.

"I'll slow down," I told Coach Shue.

The coach smiled. "Terrific!" she said. "I think we'll do great in the competition!"

"Me, too," I said, but I felt my heart sinking.

CHAPTER 8

NO MORE CAPTAIN

After practice, I walked to Ava's house. I stood on the front lawn for a few minutes, remembering how we had practiced and laughed there before tryouts. I took a deep breath and walked to the door.

The door opened as soon as I rang the doorbell, and Ava stood on the other side. She was smiling a wide smile, but it disappeared as soon as she realized it was me.

I spoke quickly, afraid she was going to close the door. "Ava, we've been friends for years, and I miss you," I said. "Coach Shue said you needed help with the cheer. Let me help you, like you helped me."

I saw tears in Ava's eyes. She brushed them away. "Yeah," she said. "I did help you. And look what happened." Then she closed the door.

I didn't want to be captain anymore. In fact, I didn't even want to be on the team. It wasn't worth it if it cost me my best friend.

* * *

The next morning, I went straight to Coach Shue's office. She smiled when she saw me.

"Can I talk to you?" I asked.

"I always have time to talk with my girls," she said, the smile still on her face.

"The thing is," I said, "I don't think I can be on the team anymore."

Her smile disappeared. "Why not?" she asked, frowning. "You're doing a great job."

Ava didn't want to be my friend, but I didn't want to tell Coach Shue that's why I was quitting. "Thank you, but it's harder than I thought it would be," I told her.

Coach Shue studied my face. "I think there's something you aren't telling me, but unless you do I can't help," she said.

"Like I said," I told her, "it's just too hard." It wasn't a lie.

CHAPTER 9

DISASTER

I was surprised to see Casey near my locker the next day. "Good, you're here!" she said.

I turned around. Maybe she was talking to someone else.

She gave me a shy smile. "I haven't been very nice the past few weeks," she said. "I'm sorry."

I nodded. "It's okay," I told her.

"Coach Shue said you quit," Casey said. "You have to come back! The routine was a disaster without you. The competition is tomorrow. We need our captain!"

"I can't do that," I said. "Ava means more to me than cheerleading."

Casey sighed. "Ava feels awful. She wants you to come back, too," she said.

I put my books in my locker and slammed it shut. "Then why isn't she here?" I asked.

"She's embarrassed," Casey explained. "After you quit, she realized that it was all her fault. She wasn't playing fair. She and Stefanie are with Coach Shue right now explaining everything."

"Really?" I asked. "You all really want me back?"

"Yep." She smiled and added, "Come on. Let's go find them. We'll fix this mess."

I still wasn't sure about seeing Ava after everything that had happened. "I don't know," I said. But Casey grabbed my arm.

As we walked down the hall, she said, "We can't win without you."

Coach Shue looked up and smiled as I walked into her office. "The team wasn't the same without you," she said. Then she looked at Ava. "I think Ava has some things to say to you. Please talk before practice."

After we left Coach Shue's office, Casey and Stefanie gave Ava and me some privacy.

"I was jealous," Ava said. "I'm sorry."

"We could have talked about it," I said.

"I know, but I just couldn't get past not being captain. And then, when I was feeling better, I was mad that I couldn't do the routine perfectly," Ava explained.

"That could have been my fault," I said. "I think I went too fast."

Ava shook her head. "No, you were perfect. I can totally see why you're captain. And," she paused, "that's what made it worse. You were going at a great pace, and I still couldn't get it. I just felt so down, especially when no one else was having trouble. So I took it out on you." She looked at the floor.

I touched her arm. "I understand," I told her. "That's how I felt when you were teaching me the moves this summer. Like I would never get them. Like you were so much better."

Ava smiled. "I'm so, so sorry. Can you forgive me?" she asked.

I pretended to think about it. Then I threw my arms around her. "Of course!" I said. "Let's always talk through things from now on, okay?"

"Always!" said Ava. Then we ran to the field arm in arm.

CHAPTER 10

THE COMPETITION

The competition was the next morning. I felt nervous at breakfast, but I ate everything. I knew I'd need the energy.

"You'll do great!" said Dad. "And I'm glad you and Ava worked things out."

"We knew you girls would work it out, though," said Mom. "You've been friends too long to ruin it over this."

After breakfast, Mom and Dad drove me to the competition site.

"Break a pom-pom!" Dad said as I got out of the car.

Mom laughed. "We'll see you out there, honey," she told me.

* * *

An hour later, the competition was in full swing. "River City East, you're up!" called one of the judges.

All the girls in our squad slapped palms and ran to the center of the gym floor.

I looked at the sea of faces in front of me, then back at my best friend and my new friends. Everyone wore huge grins. "Ready? Okay!" I yelled.

We launched into the Hello cheer. When the time came to throw our pom-poms in the air and catch them again, my stomach did a little flip. But we all did it.

We each landed on our feet and caught our pom-poms. Ava's smile was bigger than I had seen it in a long time.

Then we got into our dance-routine formation. When we were ready, I gave Coach Shue a small nod. She started the music. We stepped out of our positions, clapping our hands. Our cartwheels and pyramid were flawless.

It felt like only seconds before it was time for the finale.

We threw our pom-poms in the air, marched into file, and fell like dominos. Not one person was out of place.

The spectators jumped out of their seats and clapped. Our group ran to the back of the gym to wait. One more group of girls performed. Then it was time for the results.

As the judge listed the winners, we all held hands. We didn't get the third-place or second-place trophy. Then the judge said, "And the first-place trophy goes to . . ." She paused as the cheers filled the gym. I held my breath. Finally, she yelled, "River City East!"

Everyone in the gym clapped, but it was hard to hear them over our screams as we jumped up and down, hugging. Coach Shue handed the trophy to me, since I was captain.

I pushed it into the center of the group. The trophy was all of ours. I wanted all our hands — especially Ava's — on the prize.

✦ ABOUT THE AUTHOR ✦

Margaret Gurevich has wanted to be a writer since second grade. She has written for many magazines and currently writes young adult and middle grade books. She lives with her husband, son, and two furry kitties, and fondly remembers her cheerleading days.

✦ ABOUT THE ILLUSTRATOR ✦

Pulsar Studio is a collection of artists from Argentina who work to bring editorial projects to life. They work with companies from different parts of the world designing characters, short stories for children, textbooks, art for book covers, comics, licensed art, and more. Images are their means of expression.

✦ GLOSSARY ✦

announcement (uh-NOUNSS-muhnt)—a public or formal notice

celebrate (SEL-uh-brate)—to do something enjoyable on a special occasion

competition (kom-puh-TISH-uhn)—a contest of some kind

direction (duh-REK-shuhn)—guidance or supervision

routine (roo-TEEN)—a regular way or pattern of doing things

squad (SKWAHD)—a small group of people involved in the same activity

transferred (TRANSS-furd)—to move from one person or place to another

tryout (TRYE-out)—a test to see if a person is qualified to do something

volume (VOL-yoom)—loudness

✦ DISCUSSION QUESTIONS ✦

1. Ava helps Julia practice before tryouts so she can learn the routines. Talk about a time you helped a friend practice for something. How did you do it?

2. What do you think are the best parts of being captain? What are the hardest parts?

3. Ava acts jealous when Julia is named captain instead of her after the cheerleading tryouts. Why do you think she was so upset?

✦ WRITING PROMPTS ✦

1. Have you ever had a friend get mad at you for an unfair reason? What happened? Write about it.

2. Stefanie tells Julia that her being captain is the best thing for the team. But it might hurt her friendship with Ava. Have you ever had to make a difficult choice like this? Write about what you would do in Julia's position.

3. Julia is nervous on her first day at a new school. Write about your first day at your school. How did you feel? What happened?

MORE ABOUT
CHEERLEADING

Want to learn more cheerleading moves? Here's some basic cheerleading terminolgy to get you started.

- **AERIAL** — a cartwheel done with no hands touching the ground; sometimes refers to a walkover or roundoff without hands.

- **BACK HANDSPRING** — a backward jump onto your hands, then a quick push from your hands to your feet.

- **BASKET TOSS** — a stunt using three or more bases, who toss a flyer into the air. Two of the bases have interlocked their hands. The flyer may do any jump in the air before returning to the cradle.

- **BUCKETS** — arms are held straight out in front of you, fists facing down as if holding the handle of a bucket in each hand.

- **CUPIE** — a base holds a flyer in one hand. The base's arm is fully extended, and both the flyer's feet are in the base's one hand.

- **FLYER** — the person who is elevated into the air by the bases; the person who is on top of a pyramid or stunt.

- **HIGH V** — a motion where both arms are locked and hands are in buckets, followed by bringing both arms up to form a V.

- **PIKE JUMP** — a jump done with both legs straight out, knees locked. Arms are in a touchdown motion out in front to create a folded position in the air.

- **SPOTTER** — a person who stays on the ground and watches for any hazards in the stunt. The spotter is responsible for watching the flyer and being prepared to catch her if she falls.